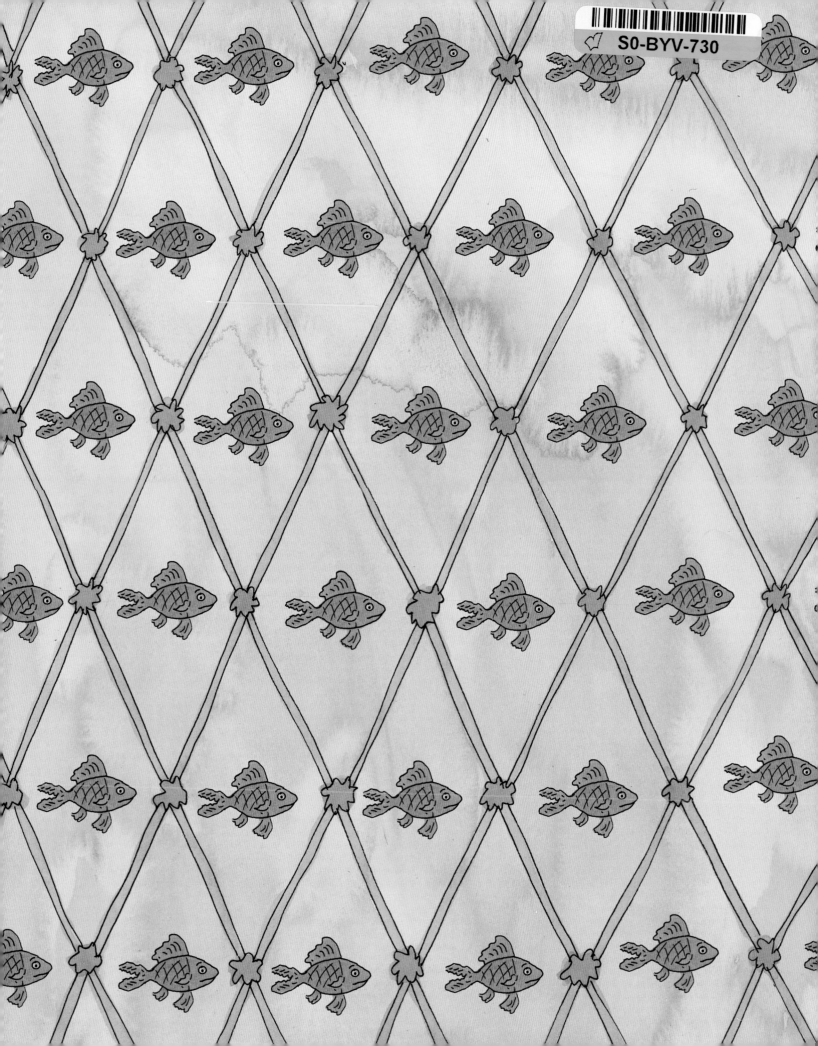

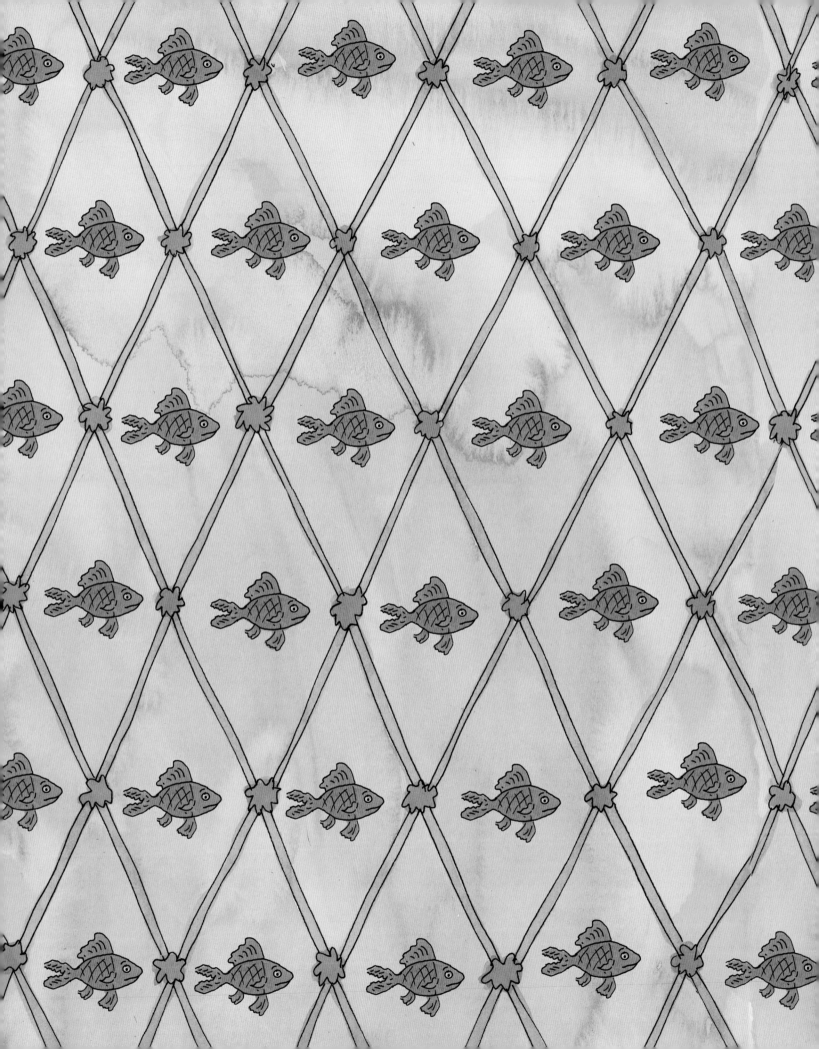

TIRED TOWN

Patty dedicates this book to Roz —P. M.

Roz dedicates this book to Patty —R. C.

Published by Roaring Brook Press
Roaring Brook Press is a division of Holtzbrinck Publishing Holdings Limited Partnership
120 Broadway, New York, NY 10271 • mackids.com

Our books may be purchased in bulk for promotional, educational, or business use. Please contact your local
bookseller or the Macmillan Corporate and Premium Sales Department at (800) 221-7945 ext. 5442
or by email at MacmillanSpecialMarkets@macmillan.com.

Library of Congress Control Number: 2022920585

First edition, 2023
The illustrations in this book were created with watercolors and finished digitally, and the type was set in
Brandon Grotesque. The book was edited by Connie Hsu and Kate Meltzer, with art direction by Sharismar
Rodriguez and Mike Burroughs and design by Mike Burroughs and Elynn Cohen. The production editor
was Kristen Stedman, and the production was supervised by Celeste Cass.
Printed in China by RR Donnelley Asia Printing Solutions Ltd., Dongguan City, Guangdong Province

ISBN 978-1-250-85912-9
1 3 5 7 9 10 8 6 4 2

TIRED TOWN

PATRICIA MARX

PICTURES BY
ROZ CHAST

Roaring Brook Press

New York

It's nighttime in Tired Town.

The spaghetti is so drained, it can't stand up straight.

The eggs are so fried, they can't keep their yolks open.

The popcorn is too pooped to pop.

And the butter? "I melted a long time ago," it says.

The buildings are so weary, they're wobbling.

The sun is so burned out, it's sinking in the sky. "Now it's your turn to shine," says the sun to the moon before disappearing below the horizon.

But there is someone in Tired Town who is not tired at all.
That would be Nellie Bee Nightly.

"My feet are wide awake," she says to the little yellow night table,
which is so tuckered out, it's flipped itself over to rest its legs.

"My mouth hasn't finished talking," she says to Cheesy, her goldfish.
Cheesy cannot talk, but if he could, he'd say, "Please keep quiet.
I'm trying to take a nap on top of my castle."

"Bye-bye," Nellie Bee says to her bed, which is sleepwalking this way and that.
"Wham-whump-thump, crash-bang-'n-bump," the bed says when it hits the wall.

"Did you hear a wham-whump-thump, crash-bang-'n-bump coming from Nellie Bee's room?" says Nellie Bee Nightly's mother. "Impossible," says her father. "Didn't she say good night hours ago?"

"Just in case, let's take a peek," her mother says.

She tiptoes to Nellie Bee's door and opens it a smidge,
careful not to wake her daughter.

Nellie Bee Nightly is jumping on the bed, yodeling the song she composed on her headboard.

Luckily, I have a flashlight, thinks Nellie Bee. There's so much to do! She must brush her teeth (with her hairbrush, of course)—

—and persuade her doll, Naked Nancy, to put on pajamas.

Cheesy could use some improvements, too.

Perhaps a fancy night bonnet?

Or a mustache.

How about some lipstick
and false eyelashes?

Or, at the very least,
a tail tutu?

And how can Nellie Bee go to sleep without giving Cheesy a bubble bath? (He insists on mozzarella scented, of course.)

And reading him a bedtime story, probably *Goodnight, Cheddar*.

But before that, Nellie Bee must teach Cheesy how to talk.

Uh-oh. What if Naked Nancy needs to go you-know-what in the middle of the night? "A walkway from the bed to the bathroom is a must-have," decides Nellie Bee.

"In case the walkway gets crowded, I must build a tunnel," she says to Cheesy.

"No, I did *not* just close my eyes," she adds, closing her eyes again. "I was practicing my slow blinking."

"I don't hear any noise coming from Nellie Bee's room," says her mother.
"She must finally be in bed," says her father.

Not exactly. Nellie Bee is hanging her bed from the ceiling to make room for the swimming pool.

And growing a tropical rain forest near the window.
Then she will build a ladder to the moon with toothpicks.

But first, she lies down on her bed. "I'm not sleeping," she says to Cheesy. "I'm pretending to be a log."

Meanwhile, Nellie Bee Nightly's socks snuggle inside her shoes, which announce they are finished walking until tomorrow.

The rug curls up and gets comfy.

The floor snores.

The books on the desk close themselves, and the characters inside close their eyes.

The blanket on the bed scooches up to kiss the pillow good night.

The moon rolls lazily onto its side.

And the lamp turns itself off.

Nellie Bee Nightly is asleep, too.
She is dreaming of a girl who is
dreaming of a girl who is dreaming
of a girl who is not tired at all.

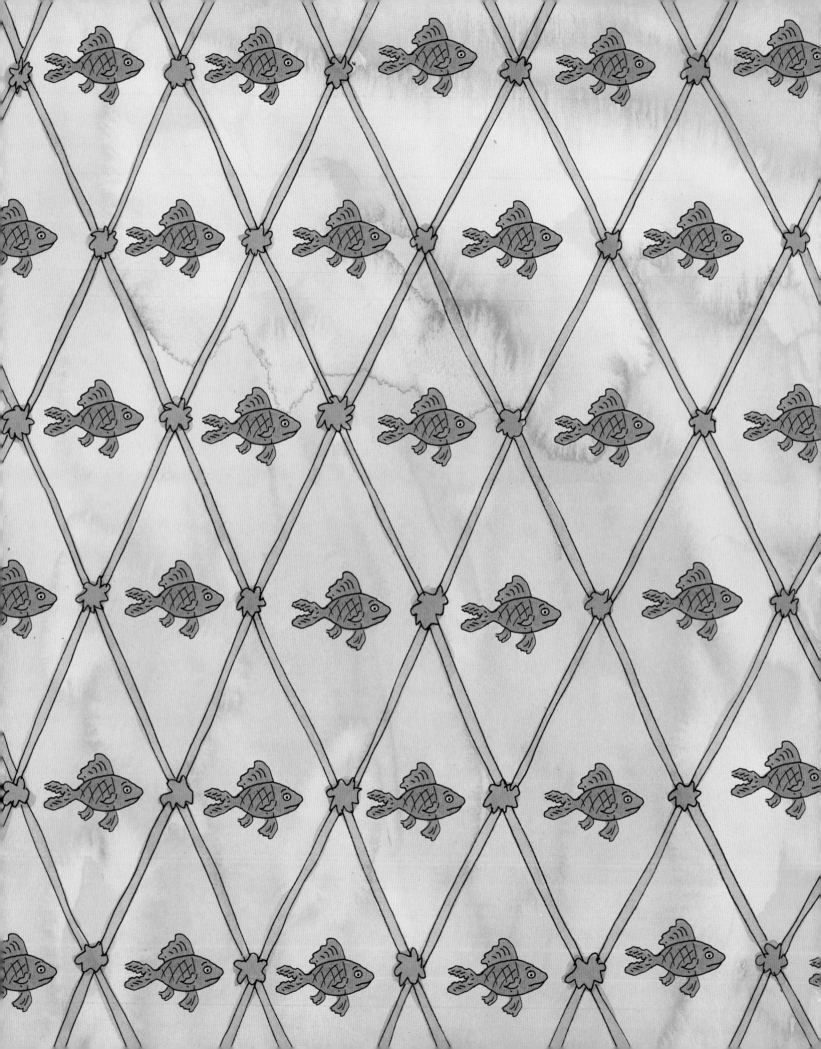